CHARACTER GUIDE

U·B·O·S ™

The Ultimate Book of Spells

CHARACTER GUIDE

By Kay Barnham

PUFFIN BOOKS

PUFFIN BOOKS

Published by the Penguin Group
Penguin Books Ltd, 80 Strand, London WC2R 0RL, England
Penguin Putnam Inc., 375 Hudson Street, New York, New York 10014, USA
Penguin Books Australia Ltd, 250 Camberwell Road, Camberwell, Victoria 3124, Australia
Penguin Books Canada Ltd, 10 Alcorn Avenue, Toronto, Ontario, Canada M4V 3B2
Penguin Books India (P) Ltd, 11 Community Centre, Panchsheel Park, New Delhi – 110 017, India
Penguin Books (NZ) Ltd, Cnr Rosedale and Airborne Roads, Albany, Auckland, New Zealand
Penguin Books (South Africa) (Pty) Ltd, 24 Sturdee Avenue, Rosebank 2196, South Africa

Penguin Books Ltd, Registered Offices: 80 Strand, London WC2R 0RL, England

www.penguin.com

First published 2002
1 3 5 7 9 10 8 6 4 2

Licensed by BKN International
UBOS™ & © 2001 BKN International AG
TV series Story Editor Sean Catherine Derek
All rights reserved

Set in Gill Sans

Made and printed in Italy by Printer Trento Srl

Except in the United States of America, this book is sold subject to the condition that it shall not,
by way of trade or otherwise, be lent, re-sold, hired out, or otherwise circulated without the
publisher's prior consent in any form of binding or cover other than that in which it is published
and without a similar condition including this condition being imposed on the subsequent
purchaser

British Library Cataloguing in Publication Data
A CIP catalogue record for this book is available from the British Library

ISBN 0–141–31474–5

Introduction

Long ago, it was foretold that an evil being would try to take over the world. It was also foretold that it would take the 'power of three' to triumph over this evil.

The Supreme Wizard, **Zarlak,** is pure evil. In 1776, he was banished by the Wizards' High Council and a furious battle followed. The Battle of All Battles had no winners. Zarlak was sent deep below the Earth's crust to Centre Earth and Supreme Wizard **Gez,** his opponent, mysteriously vanished.

Zarlak is still imprisoned and he has only one mission. He needs to steal enough magic to set him free from Centre Earth. Then he plans to make a triumphant return to Surface Earth to take over the whole world!

But the Wizards' High Council has a secret weapon. The Ultimate Book of Spells – **UBOS.** An incredibly magical book, UBOS has the power to travel between Surface Earth and Centre Earth. UBOS does not go alone. He takes three magical beings with him to fight the Supreme Wizard – three students from Vonderland School.

Vonderland School is a perfectly normal school in the German city of Hamburg – until you look behind the Veil of Illusion … Here, young witches and wizards are taught the magical tricks of the trade. They learn how to transform themselves into different beings, how to fly a Scootsoomer, how to mix potions, cast spells and even how to make themselves invisible. Cassy, Gus and Verne are students at Vonderland.

Thirteen-year-old **Cassy** is a talented student, a Scootsoomer champion and a fearless leader. She is the great-grandaughter of Supreme Wizard Gez and a junior witch who always comes top of her class.

Twelve-year-old **Gus** is a junior wizard from a long line of wizards and sorceresses. His father is a pure elf and his mother is a sorceress. Gus is worried that he will never match up to his fantastic family, but all he needs to do is believe in himself.

Eleven-year-old **Verne** is the only child of good-natured Mortie-Mud parents, who have no idea that magic really exists in the world. He finds it hard to get his logical mind around the idea of magic. He keeps thinking that he will wake up to discover that his life at Vonderland is just a dream.

Together, the junior witch, apprentice wizard and gifted Mortie make up 'the power of three' that was foretold long, long ago. With UBOS, it is their job to make sure that evil magic never takes over the world.

It won't be easy.

The
Good

CASSY

Being:

Junior witch

Accessories:

Wand, SCOOTSOOMER, backpack

Magical powers:

CASSY can't help being brilliant at magic – she is the 56th generation of a family of famous witches and wizards. And no one can beat her on a SCOOTSOOMER.

Realms:

Vonderland

Relationship:

The Supreme Wizard, GEZ, is CASSY's great-grandfather.

Adventures:

Whenever there is mystery or adventure in the air, CASSY is the first to suggest a trip to Centre Earth to sort it out. Quick-thinking and fast-talking, nothing scares the junior witch – even WYRMOST, the most terrifying dragon ever!

GUS HANDSOFF

Being:

Half-elf apprentice wizard

Accessories:

Wand, SCOOTSOOMER

Magical powers:

Wiggles his ears and talks to tree dwellers

Realms:

Vonderland

Relationship:

ALEC HANDSOFF'S younger brother and MR HANDSOFF's son

Adventures:

GUS is one cool dude who's always ready for a trip to Centre Earth. At first, he's suspicious of VERNE, but soon realizes that the power of three (CASSY, VERNE and him) is a force to be reckoned with! Together, they can outwit the most evil wizard of all time – ZARLAK.

VERNE WIGHARD

Being:
Gifted Mortie (a human who believes in magic)

Accessories:
Antenna wand, SCOOTSOOMER named Ambrose

Magical powers:
VERNE is a techno-wizard — he can add magic to any objects with his antenna wand.

Realms:
Vonderland

Relationship:
Descendant of MERLIN AMBROSIUS and son of Mr and Mrs Wighard

Adventures:
Since coming to Vonderland, VERNE's whole life has been one long adventure. UBOS regularly takes him, CASSY and GUS down to Centre Earth to fight against evil. He doesn't really want to be part of the magical world of Vonderland, but he knows that CASSY and GUS need him — to defeat ZARLAK.

UBOS

Being:

Magical book called
The Ultimate Book
of Spells

Accessories:

Pages packed with facts
about all things magical –
and thousands of spells!

Magical powers:

The ability to whizz CASSY,
GUS and VERNE down to
Centre Earth

Realms:

Vonderland

Relationship:

UBOS is very closely related to the Supreme Wizard, GEZ …

Adventures:

UBOS's pages are the ticket to adventure and knowledge. Without
him, CASSY, GUS and VERNE would be powerless against the evil
in Centre Earth. And it's not easy being the Ultimate Book of
Spells. UBOS has to cope with losing his logic, falling apart at the
seams, being frozen and ending up in the clutches of the evil
ZARLAK …

ALEC HANDSOFF

Being: Half-elf sorcerer

Accessories: Wand

Magical powers: ALEC has just passed his magical exams. He has a wand and he knows how to use it!

Realms: Germany

Relationship: GUS HANDSOFF's popular and very good-looking older brother

Adventures: ALEC is the leader of the OMM (Open Magic Movement). He wants to allow Enchanteds (witches, wizards and other magical beings) to practise magic amongst Mortie-Muds. But magic can be frightening to people who don't understand what's happening …

COACH KUBA

Being: Half-human, half-zebra

Accessories: Magical hourglass

Magical powers: Changes into human form

Realms: Vonderland

Relationship: Teaches SCOOTSOOMER and PE at Vonderland

Adventures: COACH KUBA is an expert at flying the SCOOTSOOMER. He hates having to change into a human when he's near Mortie-Muds. He'd rather the world sees him for what he is.

CUPID

Being: Roman god of love

Accessories: Magic bow – pink for love and blue to reverse

Magical powers: CUPID has the power to make people fall in love.

Realms: World of the Imps

Relationship: CUPID is now retired.

Adventures: When CUPID's bow falls into CASSY's hands, she accidentally makes the Vonderland staff and pupils fall in love with each other. It's up to CUPID to put the magic right – but the god of love has had enough of romance ... he's a bouncer in a club at the Heartbreak Hotel!

DR MENDER

Being: Half-goat, half-human

Accessories: Potions and medicines to cure sick and injured animals

Magical powers: Heals enchanted creatures at the Vonderland Sanctuary

Realms: Vonderland

Relationship: CASSY loves animals – she is one of DR MENDER's most eager students.

Adventures: As Bestial Physician, DR MENDER is kept busy at Vonderland. He teaches Magical Botany and Implementing Mystical Enchantments, while taking care of enchanted creatures in the Vonderland Sanctuary.

ELFIN

Being: European wood elf

Accessories: None

Magical powers: Flying

Realms: Vonderland

Relationship: ELFIN guards the Vonderland dormitories. He tries to make sure that no one sneaks in – or out! However, he has a bit of a crush on Cassy, and she has been known to sweet-talk her way round him.

Adventures: Tough, tiny and very, very nosey, ELFIN just can't help being involved in CASSY, GUS and VERNE's adventures.

ELSA

Being: Frost giantess

Accessories: None

Magical powers: Super strong!

Realms: Vonderland

Relationship: ELSA's parents are MAMA and PAPA. Her uncle is YMIR.

Adventures: It's not easy for a 3.5-metre-tall frost giantess to fit in at Vonderland – especially when LUCREZIA is involved. ELSA runs away and falls straight into ZARLAK's trap. Another job for CASSY, GUS and VERNE!

ERBERT

Being: Royal Toad

Accessories: Golden crown and wind-up key

Magical powers: The power to annoy anyone!

Realms: Vonderland

Relationship: CASSY, GUS and VERNE's toy mascot

Adventures: ERBERT was once a toad prince who loved to make fun of people – until a powerful old crone called GOODY TOOTHPICKS decided to teach him a lesson. She turned him into a toy, so that he would make other people laugh. Cowardly and stammering, ERBERT does not like danger. But he always comes to the rescue if he is really needed.

FLAHERTY

Being: Irish leprechaun

Accessories: The luck of the Irish!

Magical powers: Mischievous magic

Realms: Leprechaun Level

Relationship: Assistant to KING NIALL – the leprechaun king

Adventures: When ZARLAK holds KING NIALL hostage, FLAHERTY asks for CASSY's help. Together, they jump into the Leprechaun Oak Tree and travel to Centre Earth to save him.

FLINK

Being: Bookbinder gnome

Accessories: Magic glue

Magical powers: The ability to repair magical books

Realms: Bookbinders' Realm

Relationship: Apprentice to FLYLEAF – head librarian

Adventures: When ZARLAK steals the books and kidnaps the bookbinder gnomes from the cavern library, FLINK manages to escape. Now it's up to him to help CASSY, GUS and VERNE defeat ZARLAK and restore the magical library.

FLORAL

Being: The Book of Floral Magic

Accessories: Pages full of magical floral spells

Magical powers: Floral magic, including the Thorn Barrier Spell

Realms: Bookbinders' Realm

Relationship: One of UBOS's friends from long ago …

Adventures: The Book of Floral Magic is beautiful, charming and very kind, with the face of a wood sprite. Her great knowledge and wisdom help VERNE just when he needs it most.

FLYLEAF

Being: Bookbinder gnome

Accessories: The gnomes' Key of Knowledge

Magical powers: Can repair any book

Realms: Bookbinders' Realm

Relationship: FLYLEAF is head librarian of the gnomes' magical library. He is also in charge of teaching FLINK how to repair magical books.

Adventures: FLYLEAF is kidnapped when ZARLAK empties the gnomes' library in search of the gnomes' Key of Knowledge. He has to rely on CASSY, GUS, VERNE and FLINK to rescue him.

GALEN

Being: Ghost

Accessories: Medical book

Magical powers: Knowledge of all things medical

Realms: Vonderland

Relationship: Once a famous Greek surgeon, GALEN's ghost now teaches at Vonderland.

Adventures: GALEN is a good old-fashioned teacher. There's nothing he doesn't know about bodies – both Mortie-Mud and magical.

GARDEN GNOMES

Being: Gnomes

Accessories: None

Magical powers: Walking, talking concrete gnomes with glowing eyes, who grow to human-size when zapped by a wand

Realms: Rootopia

Relationship: Controlled by ZARLAK

Adventures: Normally harmless concrete figures, the GARDEN GNOMES are now in ZARLAK's power. In order to steal magic from above the Earth's crust, he forces the gnomes to pull the flowers from Surface World down into Rootopia – by their roots!

GARG

Being: Gargoyle

Accessories: All-seeing eyes

Magical powers: Can magically move from place to place

Realms: Vonderland

Relationship: A school guard

Adventures: Garg is a silent, but important, being at Vonderland. He guards the upper towers, watching over the school grounds. Watch out for him – he moves around!

GEZ

Being: Supreme Wizard

Accessories: Magic staff with Valdar crystal

Magical powers: Most powerful wizard since Merlin

Realms: Everywhere …

Relationship: He is now UBOS!

Adventures: When ZARLAK was banished to Centre Earth, the only way that GEZ could survive was to transform himself into a book – the Ultimate Book of Spells. As UBOS, his mission is to help CASSY, GUS and VERNE to remove ZARLAK's power altogether. But his identity must remain a secret. If CASSY were ever to find out who UBOS really is, it would put her life in danger … Meanwhile, a banquet is held at Vonderland every year to honour GEZ and his amazing achievements!

GRIFFEN

Being: Half-lion, half-eagle

Accessories: Huge wings

Magical powers: Enchanted creature

Realms: Vonderland

Relationship: Lives at Vonderland Sanctuary, under DR MENDER's care

Adventures: GRIFFEN is affected by one of ZARLAK's spells – a crash bug that makes him fall out of the sky …

GRIMWEED

Being: Digital game wizard

Accessories: Wand

Magical powers: None

Realms: Surface World

Relationship: GRIMWEED is not real – he's just a pixel image created by VERNE for his computer game.

Adventures: Instead of doing what he's been programmed to do, GRIMWEED suddenly starts behaving really oddly. He pulls faces and blows raspberries at VERNE instead of taking part in his computer game. It's all because logic is being drained from Surface World down to Logikus Null.

GROK

Being: Ogre

Accessories: Fierce expression

Magical powers: Very strong and agile for his size

Realms: Oversize Realm

Relationship: WITCH CASSANDRA the SEVENTH'S right-hand ogre

Adventures: Gruff and frightening, but with a hero's heart, GROK would never let CASSANDRA down.

HEADLY

Being: Floating bust

Accessories: None

Magical powers: Psychic

Realms: Vonderland

Relationship: One of CASSY, GUS and VERNE's friends

Adventures: HEADLY is one of the first beings VERNE meets when he arrives at Vonderland. A dreadful gossip, the statue often panics and passes fear on to others.

HEADMISTRESS CRYSTALGAZER

Being: Sorceress

Accessories: Magic golden skeleton key that has the power to unlock almost any spell ... including the one keeping Zarlak in Centre Earth

Magical powers: Spends much of her time as a red cat, but pops back into human form when she is cross or upset

Realms: Vonderland

Relationship: The charming, attractive ROLAND DARTMOOR is HEADMISTRESS CRYSTALGAZER's nephew.

Adventures: The Vonderland headmistress teaches Vanishing Class, Levitations and the Rules of Magical Ethics. A member of the Wizards' High Council, HEADMISTRESS CRYSTALGAZER is firmly on the side of the good guys. Does she know about UBOS, or doesn't she ...?

JACK O'LANTERN

Being: Enchanted pumpkin

Accessories: Wings

Magical powers: Can fly and talk

Realms: Vonderland

Relationship: Takes part in a SCOOTSOOMER game

Adventures: Wizard Squash 'Em is a type of tennis played on SCOOTSOOMERs. The Jack O'Lantern acts as a ball. A net hangs magically in the air between the two players as they hit the talkative pumpkin back and forth.

KING NIALL

Being: Irish leprechaun king

Accessories: Shillelagh – wooden stick used as a weapon, pot of gold

Magical powers: Turns rocks into gold

Realms: Leprechaun Level

Relationship: One of CASSY's friends

Adventures: ZARLAK really has it in for KING NIALL. First he holds the leprechaun king to ransom, then he steals his pot of gold. It's up to CASSY, GUS and VERNE to help the king out.

LAVA MEN

Beings: Lava dwellers

Accessories: Flame hair

Magical powers: Control the temperature of the world's lava flow

Realms: Fornax

Relationship: Work for ZARLAK – against their will

Adventures: These fiery creatures live in the hottest part of Centre Earth. Forced by ZARLAK to take part in one of his evil plans, he makes them halt the moon during a solar eclipse so that it stays in front of the sun. Soon, everyone and everything (including the world's magic) starts to freeze …

LITERAL BUG

Being: Enchanted insect

Accessories: Crystal cage

Magical powers: Makes its victim's words come true. For example, when GUS says that something seems 'fishy', he's immediately surrounded by fish flopping around on the floor.

Realms: Vonderland

Relationship: Lives in the Vonderland Sanctuary under DR MENDER's care

Adventures: The LITERAL BUG is a timid creature that just wants to be left alone. But, when LUCREZIA and BORGE set the LITERAL BUG free, it fights back with one of the most powerful forces of all – words!

MADAME CURIE

Being: Ghost

Accessories: A great scientific mind

Magical powers: Ghostly magic

Realms: Vonderland

Relationship: Teaches the Potions class at Vonderland

Adventures: Madame Curie is the brilliant scientist who discovered radium. As a ghost, she passes on her knowledge to students at Vonderland.

MAGICAL CARPET OF CARBALLEY

Being: Enchanted carpet

Accessories: Tassels for steering

Magical powers: Can fly

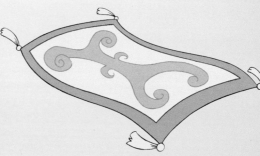

Realms: Centre Earth and Vonderland

Relationship: Freed from ZARLAK by CASSY, GUS and VERNE

Adventures: Expertly piloted by GUS, the carpet is rescued from the clutches of ZARLAK.

MAGUS

Being: Wizard

Accessories: Crystal ball

Magical powers: MAGUS is very small and timid.

Realms: Level of Illusion

Relationship: Master of illusions

Adventures: Wizard MAGUS specializes in illusions. He can turn himself into an enormous, terrifying figure with glowing eyes to scare people, when he is really very tiny. Although Magus conjures up some nasty illusions to protect his level from Zarlak, he is not an evil being.

MAMA and PAPA

Beings: Frost giants

Accessories: None

Magical powers: Able to perform magic

Realms: Jotenheim Estates

Relationship: ELSA's parents

Adventures: MAMA and PAPA are very proud of ELSA. They can't believe it when she is rude to YMIR, her own uncle, and hurls him out of Vonderland . . . MAMA and PAPA blame Vonderland for teaching her bad manners and spells — they threaten to attack the school, unless YMIR is found, safe and sound.

MASTER COAT-OF-ARMS

Being: Enchanted coat

Accessories: Ten arms

Magical powers:
All students' family trees are imprinted
on his memory.

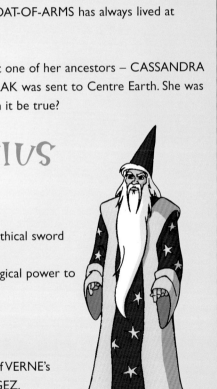

Realms: Vonderland

Relationship: The MASTER COAT-OF-ARMS has always lived at
Vonderland.

Adventures: He tells CASSY that one of her ancestors – CASSANDRA
the SEVENTH – vanished the day that ZARLAK was sent to Centre Earth. She was
a traitor! CASSY can't believe her ears – can it be true?

MERLIN AMBROSIUS

Being: Greatest wizard of all time

Accessories: Excalibur – the mythical sword

Magical powers: Has the magical power to
do anything!

Realms: Everywhere!

Relationship: MERLIN is one of VERNE's
ancestors. He also taught Supreme Wizard GEZ.

Adventures: Long ago, King Arthur was
guided by the wisdom and magical feats of Supreme
Wizard MERLIN. Now, MERLIN appears once again. He must help CASSY, GUS
and VERNE to break the spell cast by SIEGE PERILOUS – the magical throne
of Sir Galahad.

MISTY

Being: Unicorn

Accessories: Magical horn

Magical powers: Touching a unicorn's horn grants wishes

Realms: DR MENDER's Sanctuary, Vonderland

Relationship: Friend of CASSY, GUS and VERNE

Adventures: When one of the ingredients CASSY needs for a secret spell is a unicorn hair, MISTY is her unlucky target.

MR HANDSOFF

Being: Elf wizard

Accessories: Flying car and very pointy ears!

Magical powers: Elfin magic

Realms: Hamburg

Relationship: GUS's father

Adventures: MR HANDSOFF is a very important elf – a member of the Elven Council. He is involved when the powers of every single elf fade away. The mystic Elvenstone, which is the source of elfin power, must be rescued from the great dragon – WYRMOST.

MR SNUBBLES

Being: Huge imaginary bunny rabbit

Accessories: Waistcoat

Magical powers: Grows to giant size, can become invisible

Realms: Whimsy Way in Centre Earth

Relationship: CASSY's imaginary friend

Adventures: The only person who can see MR SNUBBLES is CASSY, because he's her imaginary friend. When ZARLAK suddenly starts stealing all of the imaginary friends and taking them to Shadowland, it's time for CASSY, GUS and VERNE to take action!

MR and MRS WIGHARD

Beings: Mortie-Muds – people who don't believe in magic

Accessories: None

Magical powers: None

Realms: Hamburg

Relationship: VERNE's father and mother

Adventures: Verne's parents can't see past the Veil of Illusion that hides Vonderland – they have no idea that it is a magical school. Even when they come to parents' day, all MR and MRS WIGHARD see is a lovely modern facility. But when ZARLAK hatches a plan to frighten VERNE's parents so much that they take him out of school, MRS WIGHARD shows that she might not be such a Mortie-Mud after all …

MS MAYDAY

Being: Banshee

Accessories: Flying hat and goggles

Magical powers: Flying ace

Realms: Vonderland

Relationship: Teaches flying and drives the Vonderland magic school bus

Adventures: MS MAYDAY loves speed and screaming, but even she is terrified when VERNE flies her into the path of a passenger jet during his SCOOTSOOMER test!

MS PROTEUS

Being: Amoeba – an animal made of just one cell

Accessories: None

Magical powers: Can transform into any object or being

Realms: Vonderland

Relationship: Teaches Magical Transformations at Vonderland

Adventures: MS PROTEUS is a wibbly-wobbly blob of a teacher at Vonderland. Her classes include Duplication, Transformations, Shape-Shifting and Magical Cooking.

PEGFORD

Being: Pegasus

Accessories: Huge wings

Magical powers: Flying horse

Realms: DR MENDER's Sanctuary at Vonderland

Relationship: One of CASSY, GUS and VERNE's friends

Adventures: PEGFORD lives at Vonderland, but loves to take to the sky. CASSY is furious when ZARLAK's crash bug makes her favourite flying horse fall to Earth. She loves all animals and is determined to stop ZARLAK's wicked spell.

PONDY

Being: Monster

Accessories: Snapping jaws with many sharp teeth!

Magical powers: Enchanted creature

Realms: Vonderland

Relationship: The Loch Ness Monster's cousin

Adventures: Scary, but harmless, PONDY lives in the depths of the Vonderland pond. He snaps at everything that comes anywhere near him, but never seems to catch anything. When ELSA's giant uncle, YMIR, arrives to visit Vonderland, he decides to go fishing. It's time for PONDY to watch out!

PRINCE BLAZE

Being: Lava dweller

Accessories: PYRO – the firefly beast

Magical powers: Able to warm himself by stepping into pools of bubbling lava

Realms: Fornax

Relationship: CASSY, GUS and VERNE's friend

Adventures: PRINCE BLAZE used to be the fiery king of the lava dwellers, until ZARLAK banished him and took over Fornax. Now all the prince wants is to have his kingdom back.

PRINCESS ESTRELLA

Being: Mystical Spanish princess

Accessories: Crystal ball, jewelled magic wand

Magical powers: Astrologer – she can read the future in the stars

Realms: Pyrenees Mountains

Relationship: Exchange student at Vonderland

Adventures: PRINCESS ESTRELLA's beauty captivates everyone at Vonderland, including VERNE. But when the princess finds out that VERNE is a Mortie, she loses interest. PRINCESS ESTRELLA is only interested in real wizards. But it's not long before the princess changes her mind.

PROFESSOR BEGELBOYCE

Being: Wizard

Accessories: A library of magical books

Magical powers: He can absorb the words from a book just by reading it – leaving the pages blank …

Realms: Vonderland

Relationship: Teaches Dead Languages and works as the Vonderland school librarian

Adventures: PROFESSOR BEGELBOYCE tells amazing stories to the Vonderland students, but VERNE realizes that he's stealing the stories from library books. It's not long before ZARLAK hears of this skill and sends a book to charm the professor into stealing the Ultimate Book of Spells – UBOS!

PROFESSOR FESTERMAN

Being: Mortie (a human who believes in magic)

Accessories: Telescope glasses

Magical powers: None

Realms: Vonderland

Relationship: Teacher at Vonderland

Adventures: PROFESSOR FESTERMAN teaches Alchemy, Astronomy and Dragon Evasion Preparedness Drill and is also in charge of the school obstacle course. He doesn't notice when one of ZARLAK's wicked spells turns everything in Surface World dull – including the thorns in his maze.

PROFESSOR GHOST

Being: Ghost

Accessories: Old-fashioned professor's outfit

Magical powers: A skilled sorcerer

Realms: Vonderland

Relationship: Teacher at Vonderland

Adventures: Tight-lipped, stern and very floaty, PROFESSOR GHOST teaches the Vonderland students Advanced Sorcery.

PROFESSOR LUDWIG

Being: Ghost

Accessories: The Golden Lyre of Orpheus

Magical powers: Plays enchanting music

Realms: Vonderland

Relationship: The ghost of Ludwig van Beethoven, the German composer, teaches music at Vonderland.

Adventures: Until CASSY, GUS and VERNE rescue PROFESSOR LUDWIG's magical lyre, the students in his class can't help playing dreadful, tuneless music.

PROFESSOR SEZ-A-ME

Being: Genie

Accessories: Magic lava lamp

Magical powers: The ability to squeeze inside his lamp

Realms: Vonderland

Relationship: Teaches at Vonderland

Adventures: PROFESSOR SEZ-A-ME, the genie of the lava lamp, teaches Wish Granting, Manual Manipulation and Snake Charming. During Wish Granting class, the professor tells CASSY, GUS and VERNE all about Charmling imps. This information comes in very handy ...

PROFESSOR STERNWAND

Being: Ghost

Accessories: Crystal ball, Moats and Monsters – an enchanted game

Magical powers: Travelling in time

Realms: Vonderland

Relationship: Teaches Magical Histories at Vonderland

Adventures: PROFESSOR STERNWAND is a transparent floating ghost whose specialist subject is the past. He shows the students exactly what happened when Supreme Wizards GEZ and ZARLAK fought each other – by taking them back to the Battle of All Battles in 1776.

PYRO

Being: Firefly beast

Accessories: None

Magical powers:
Can withstand fiery temperatures

Realms: Fornax

Relationship: PRINCE BLAZE's trusty steed

Adventures: Even though PRINCE BLAZE is no longer king of the lava dwellers, PYRO stands by his master.

QWILL

Being: Charmling imp

Accessories: Ring of the Blue Moon

Magical powers: Grants wishes

Realms: Charmling Realm

Relationship: The brave leader of the Charmling imp resistance

Adventures: Even though ZARLAK has banned the Charmling imps from granting wishes, QWILL and the other imps are determined to continue. They must also stop ZARLAK from finding the Ring of the Blue Moon – a ring so powerful that it can free the Supreme Wizard from Centre Earth ...

RAGAMUFFIN

Being: Floppy-eared hound dog

Accessories: Huge floppy ears!

Magical powers: Can change shape and become invisible

Realms: Whimsy Way in Centre Earth

Relationship: VERNE's imaginary friend

Adventures: The only person who can see RAGAMUFFIN is VERNE, because he's his imaginary friend. When ZARLAK suddenly starts stealing all of the imaginary friends and taking them to Shadowland, it's time for CASSY, GUS and VERNE to bring their old friends to life.

SCOOTSOOMER

Being: Magical broomstick and scooter – in one!

Accessories: Motorbike handlebars – twist them to fly faster; seat cushion can be used as a flotation device; power gem makes the SCOOTSOOMER fly

Magical powers: Shrinks to fit into the owner's pocket

Realms: Vonderland

Relationship: Every Vonderland student has a SCOOTSOOMER.

Adventures: Witches and wizards used to fly on broomsticks – now they have SCOOTSOOMERs! Students at Vonderland are taught to fly fast and furiously, and they must pass a driving test. CASSY is a SCOOTSOOMER champion – no one can beat her.

SCRIMPY

Being: Imp

Accessories: Exceedingly long eyebrows

Magical powers: Impish sense of humour

Realms: World of the Imps

Relationship: CASSY, GUS and VERNE's naughty friend

Adventures: SCRIMPY is a small, bad tempered and mischievous imp who loves practical jokes. He comes to ask CASSY, GUS and VERNE for help when ZARLAK threatens to take over the World of the Imps.

SHIMMARYN

Being: Undersea Kelpie stallion

Accessories: None

Magical powers: The power to live underwater

Realms: Undersea Realm

Relationship: CASSY's friend

Adventures: SHIMMARYN is a prisoner of the SELKIES, inside the KRAKEN prison … CASSY asks this noble beast to help her in order to set him and the other sea creatures free.

SIRENS 'N' CHANT

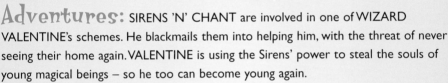

Beings: Sirens

Accessories: Magic trailer – the inside is decorated like a Greek temple

Magical powers: Steal souls

Realms: Vonderland

Relationship: Helena, Minerva and Europa make up the girl band, SIRENS 'N' CHANT.

Adventures: SIRENS 'N' CHANT are involved in one of WIZARD VALENTINE's schemes. He blackmails them into helping him, with the threat of never seeing their home again. VALENTINE is using the Sirens' power to steal the souls of young magical beings – so he too can become young again.

SKELETON

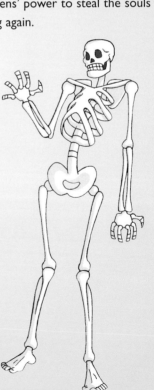

Being: Skeleton

Accessories: Bones

Magical powers: Floating collection of bones

Realms: Vonderland

Relationship: Rattles around the school

Adventures: SKELETON is one of the oldest residents of Vonderland.

SNAP

Being: Dwarf dragon

Accessories: Post bag

Magical powers: Can fly and breathe fire

Realms: Surface World

Relationship: Delivers mail to students at Vonderland

Adventures: SNAP delivers many enchanted parcels, but the most important is a special delivery for CASSY – the Ultimate Book of Spells!

SPARKY

Being: Living star

Accessories: Bright light

Magical powers: Brilliantly shiny

Realms: Whimsy Way in Centre Earth

Relationship: GUS's imaginary friend

Adventures: The only person who would have a star for an imaginary friend is GUS – elves love sparkly, shiny things. When ZARLAK suddenly starts taking all of the imaginary friends to Shadowland, it's time for CASSY, GUS and VERNE to return them to where they belong!

STUDENTS

Beings: Ghouls, witches, wizards, elves and other magical beings

Accessories: Wands, SCOOTSOOMERs

Magical powers: Beginner magic

Realms: Vonderland

Relationship: Students at Vonderland

Adventures: The students of Vonderland mustn't know about CASSY, GUS and VERNE's adventures in Centre Earth. And they must never find out about UBOS …

SUGAR PLUM FAIRIES

Being: Fairies

Accessories: Gossamer wings

Magical powers: Fairy magic

Realms: Vonderland

Relationship: They help out at Vonderland.

Adventures: Beautiful, not practical, the SUGAR PLUM FAIRIES are lovely to look at, but about as useful as a chocolate cauldron.

TALKING FLOWERS

Beings: Begonia, forget-me-not, tulip, petunia, violet and sunflower

Accessories: Pretty petals

Magical powers: Ability to talk

Realms: Vonderland

Relationship: CASSY's friends

Adventures: CASSY often waters the enchanted garden at Vonderland. When the TALKING FLOWERS start to disappear, she is worried. Then she finds out that ZARLAK is to blame …

TOOTH FAIRY

Being: Fairy

Accessories: Fairy wand, gossamer wings, sparkly tiara

Magical powers: Karate expert, flies at the speed of light, ability to travel between realms

Realms: Surface World

Relationship: One of UBOS's friends

Adventures: BAGS and BOODLES decide to kidnap the TOOTH FAIRY and hold her to ransom, but they get more trouble than they bargained for. The TOOTH FAIRY can certainly stand up for herself!

WINGED LION

Being: Mythical creature

Accessories: Huge wings

Magical powers: Flies like a bird

Realms: DR MENDER's Sanctuary at Vonderland

Relationship: Under care of DR MENDER

Adventures: CASSY visits the WINGED LION and the other creatures in DR MENDER's Sanctuary.

WITCH CASSANDRA the SEVENTH

Being: Sorceress

Accessories: Wand

Magical powers: The power to hold ZARLAK at bay

Realms: Oversize Realm – Cassandra's stronghold

Relationship: CASSY's great-aunt and one of UBOS's great friends

Adventures: CASSANDRA the SEVENTH's portrait is not displayed in the Vonderland Hall of Honour because she is thought to be a traitor. Was she really on ZARLAK's side, or has she been fighting for the good guys all along …?

YMIR

Being: Frost giant

Accessories: Great sense of humour

Magical powers: Incredible strength

Realms: Jotenheim Estates

Relationship: ELSA's uncle

Adventures: Goofy, playful, huge and oafish, YMIR is a really big frost giant. He comes to Vonderland to see his favourite niece, but ELSA isn't pleased to see him. YMIR is so embarrassing! By sending him away, ELSA gives ZARLAK the chance to stir up trouble between Vonderland and the frost giants.

GOOD REALMS

BOOKBINDERS' REALM

Features: Huge underground cavern library filled with magical books — and bookbinding gnomes who know how to repair them!

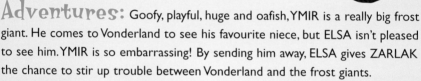

Dwellers: FLINK, FLYLEAF and many other bookbinding gnomes; FLORAL – The Great Book of Floral Magic

Magical objects: The gnomes' Key of Knowledge – the key that unlocks the magic from the gnomes' magical library

Adventures: ZARLAK knows that the gnomes' Key of Knowledge unlocks the magic from the magical library. He will stop at nothing to get it.

GOOD REALMS

CHARMLING REALM

Features: In the Charmling Realm all wishes come true.

Dwellers: Charmling imps – when they use their wish-granting power, sparks fly from their ears

Magical objects: Ring of the Blue Moon – a ring so powerful that it can grant any wish

Adventures: ZARLAK goes to the Charmling Realm to steal the Ring of the Blue Moon from QWILL, the leader of the Charmling resistance. He plans to use its wish-granting power to free himself from Centre Earth on the night of the blue moon …

FORNAX

Features: Hissing geysers and bubbling lava streams

Dwellers: LAVA MEN, PRINCE BLAZE, PYRO

Magical objects: Sandpo – a magical device from Scandinavian mythology

Adventures: When ZARLAK discovers Sandpo, he uses it to focus magic on the solar eclipse, holding the moon in front of the sun. Slowly, steadily, everything in Surface World begins to freeze. If the Wizards' High Council freezes, ZARLAK will be free!

LEVEL OF ILLUSION

Features: Fortress, leprechaun prison colony

Dwellers: MAGUS; fantastical creatures that are really just make-believe

Magical objects: When the Veil of Illusion is stolen from Vonderland, it is taken here.

Adventures: In the Level of Illusion nothing is as it seems. Everything is fake – even the fortress is just scenery, as if it's part of a film set. When MAGUS steals the Veil of Illusion to hide his level from ZARLAK, Vonderland can be seen by Mortie-Muds. CASSY, GUS and VERNE must help MAGUS and hide Vonderland, before it's too late!

OVERSIZE REALM

Features: WITCH CASSANDRA the SEVENTH's secret stronghold

Dwellers: WITCH CASSANDRA the SEVENTH, GROK

Magical objects: Oversized plants and giant insects

Adventures: Inside the Oversize Realm is a magnificent cathedral cavern where CASSY's great-aunt plots against ZARLAK. One day, he will be beaten!

The
Bad

ZARLAK

Being: The most evil wizard of all time

Accessories: Magic staff with built-in crystal ball; huge, scary castle with lava moat

Magical powers:

Fires beams of blinding energy

Realms:

Centre Earth

Relationship:

Everyone's enemy – almost!

Adventures:

ZARLAK is the ultimate bad guy. Over two hundred years ago, he was banished from Surface World by the Wizards' High Council. Ever since, he has been trying to steal the world's magic to free himself from Centre Earth. It's up to CASSY, GUS, VERNE and UBOS to stop him!

ROWCE and SNERRAT

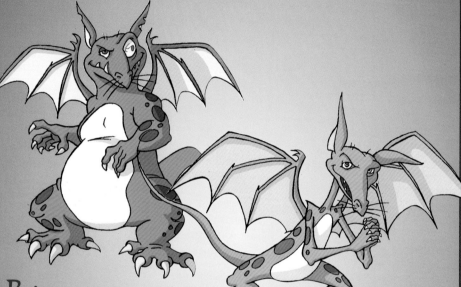

Being: Ratfinkles – rodent-imps

Accessories: Scaly wings

Magical powers:
They can fly and – with a wave of ZARLAK's staff – they turn into the
GIANT TWO-HEADED RATFINKLE.

Realms: Centre Earth

Relationship: ZARLAK's servants

Adventures:
Sneaky, spiteful and very naughty, ROWCE and SNERRAT are Centre
Earth's comic duo. They would love to escape ZARLAK's clutches –
but they are completely under his control. And the Supreme Wizard
forces his ratfinkles to follow CASSY, GUS and VERNE in attempts to
steal UBOS, time and time again …

GIANT TWO-HEADED RATFINKLE

Being:
Giant dragon-like beast

Accessories:
Fiery breath!

Magical powers:
Can fly

Realms:
Centre Earth

Relationship:
ZARLAK creates this monster from ROWCE and SNERRAT.

Adventures:
ROWCE and SNERRAT can't stand each other, so they hate it when ZARLAK waves his magic staff to turn them both into the GIANT TWO-HEADED RATFINKLE. But ZARLAK knows that this huge monster is enough to scare anyone.

BORGE and LUCREZIA

Being: Junior wizard and witch

Accessories: Wands, SCOOTSOOMERs

Magical powers: Student-level magic

Realms: Vonderland

Relationship: Twin brother and sister – CRUCALLOUS is their father

Adventures: BORGE and LUCREZIA think they're really cool – so why are CASSY, GUS and VERNE the popular ones? What's their secret? The twins will stop at nothing to show everyone that they are the best – by cheating, lying and performing illegal magic. They will even go so far as helping ZARLAK …

BAGS and BOODLES

Being: Scavenger imps

Accessories: The dream wand of Lemuria – used to steal dreams; they own a shop in a bazaar

Magical powers: Scavenger imps are small, crafty creatures, who spend their time stealing treasures from the different realms in Centre Earth. The imps sell the stolen goods in their shop. They are also skilled pickpockets.

Realms: World of the Imps

Relationship: Brothers

Adventures: BAGS and BOODLES 'find' a magic portal to Surface World, sneak through it and steal goods from under the Mortie-Muds' noses! They help Zarlak to steal dreams. Worst of all, they hold the Tooth Fairy to ransom for one million unmarked gold dubloons …

COCKROACH BEAST

Being: Giant insect

Accessories: Huge, snapping jaws

Magical powers: Amazing strength

Realms: Bookbinders' Realm

Relationship: Controlled by ZARLAK

Adventures: Once a normal insect, this cockroach was zapped by ZARLAK and transformed into the enormous COCKROACH BEAST. His job is to help ROWCE and SNERRAT to steal the gnomes' Key of Knowledge.

CRUCALLOUS

Being: Wizard

Accessories: Private vault of horrors, exotic pet shop, flying hearse

Magical powers: Very powerful and very evil wizard

Realms: Surface World

Relationship: BORGE and LUCREZIA's father

Adventures: When ZARLAK was banished to Centre Earth, CRUCALLOUS was lucky not to be sent with him. Now, he makes a living by selling endangered and exotic animals in his pet shop. BORGE and LUCREZIA help him by stealing animals. But CRUCALLOUS is playing a risky game. If the Wizards' High Council finds out what he's been doing, this time they won't let him off so lightly …

GALK

Being: Shadow goblin

Accessories: None

Magical powers: Shape-shifts into Carl, a handsome Mortie magician

Realms: Shadowland

Relationship: ZARLAK's servant

Adventures: GALK takes part in ZARLAK's evil plan to steal shadows, dragging them kicking and screaming down to Shadowland. The Supreme Wizard knows that shadows contain powerful magic. He can use these to free himself from Centre Earth.

GIANT ONE-EYED OGRE

Being: Ogre

Accessories: Club

Magical powers: Enormous strength

Realms: Centre Earth

Relationship: One of a group of many ogres

Adventures: The GIANT ONE-EYED OGRE is the only one left behind when SIRENS 'N' CHANT sing to him and his friends. Is this because he couldn't hear the enchanting singing?

GIANT TWO-HEADED CAT

Being: Giant two-headed cat

Accessories: Red collar

Magical powers: Enormous strength and speed

Realms: Leprechaun Level

Relationship: Created by ZARLAK

Adventures: When KING NIALL is held hostage by ZARLAK, the GIANT TWO-HEADED CAT makes sure that he doesn't even think of escaping.

GNOB

Being: Troll

Accessories: None

Magical powers: Beginner magic

Realms: Vonderland

Relationship: BORGE and LUCREZIA's friend

Adventures: GNOB is the only troll at Vonderland, so rather than risk being bullied, he hangs around with the twins and bullies other students instead. However, it takes a troll to catch a troll and when the GOLD TROLLS steal VERNE, GNOB's help is needed.

GOLD TROLLS

Beings: Trolls

Accessories: Golden trinkets

Magical powers: Speak in rhyme

Realms: Troll Realm

Relationship: One of many troll tribes in Centre Earth

Adventures: When GUS accidentally turns VERNE into solid gold, the gold trolls can't resist the Mortie wizard and carry him off to their home. VERNE must be rescued before sunset, or he will be melted into liquid gold and turned into a golden troll.

GOODY TOOTHPICKS

Being: Crone

Accessories: Cauldron

Magical powers: Casts powerful spells

Realms: Umbra

Relationship: Turned ERBERT into a toy

Adventures: GOODY TOOTHPICKS fights huge beasts bare-handed and then uses their bones for toothpicks. Years ago, she turned ERBERT into a toy because he laughed at her. She is thoroughly evil.

GORGON HEADS

Being: Illusion

Accessories: Spear

Magical powers: None

Realms: MAGUS's castle of illusion

Relationship: Guards castle entrance

Adventures: Half-women, half-serpents, with snakes instead of hair, the GORGON HEADS are two of the magical illusions that decorate MAGUS's castle of illusion. He tries to make the Level of Illusion a terrifying place, so no one will ever attack.

HARRIER

Being: Evil creature; half-woman, half-hawk

Accessories: Huge wings and talons

Magical powers: Can fly

Realms: Centre Earth

Relationship: One of ZARLAK's servants

Adventures: HARRIER will do anything for ZARLAK …

KRAKEN

Being: Coral reef octopus

Accessories: Huge tentacles

Magical powers: Amazing strength

Realms: Centre of the sea

Relationship: KRAKEN watches over the SELKIES' Undersea Realm.

Adventures: At first glance, KRAKEN looks like a towering rock dome held up by arching pillars. It's not until CASSY, GUS and VERNE are inside that they realize it's really a giant octopus …

LORD SELKAR

Being: Selkie

Accessories: None

Magical powers:
Conjures up the magic of the sea, can shape-shift

Realms: Undersea Realm

Relationship: Leader of the SELKIES

Adventures: LORD SELKAR appears as a sea captain to lure GUS away from Vonderland. When CASSY comes to find her friend, she is swirled down into SELKAR's underwater world.

MASTER WIZARD VALENTINE

Being: Wizard

Accessories: Wand

Magical powers:
The power to change himself from an ancient-looking wizard to a young, handsome charmer

Realms: Surface World

Relationship:
One of ZARLAK's friends

Adventures: VALENTINE persuades CASSY and GUS that they could be great if they had the Tear of Moolana from the Cave of Neveria. He goes on to manage SIRENS 'N' CHANT – using the girl band to help him stay forever young.

MINI MITES

Being: Sprite-like creatures

Accessories: Sparkles

Magical powers: Power to bring objects to life

Realms: Rootopia, Vonderland

Relationship: Released by ZARLAK

Adventures: The mini-mites are so tiny that the only way to spot them is by the sparkle of their wings. But the damage they create is huge! ZARLAK sends them to Vonderland, and the chaos begins.

NAP

Being: Dwarf dragon

Accessories: Post bag

Magical powers: Can fly and breathe fire

Realms: Surface World, Centre Earth

Relationship: Under ZARLAK's control

Adventures: NAP delivered the post with SNAP, until he was sacked. His first job for ZARLAK is to frighten MR and MRS WIGHARD – in an attempt to make them take VERNE away from Vonderland.

NEELO

Being: Charmling imp

Accessories: Magical ears

Magical powers: Grants wishes

Realms: Charmling Realm

Relationship: Betrays the Charmling
imps to ZARLAK

Adventures: NEELO tells ZARLAK
that the Ring of the Blue Moon is so powerful, the Supreme Wizard could wish
himself free from Centre Earth forever!

ONE-EYED GIANT SWAMP SLUG BEAST

Being: Giant slug

Accessories: Heaps of sticky goo

Magical powers: Enchanted creature

Realms: Underworld Swamp Realm

Relationship: ZARLAK's watchdog

Adventures: The animals in
DR MENDER's Sanctuary are suffering from
ZARLAK's crash bug – they can't fly. The only
cure is Slime Rooters – and these can only be
found in the Underworld Swamp Realm. The
SWAMP BEAST's job is to stop CASSY, GUS and
VERNE finding the Slime Rooters.

PUCK

Being: Sprite

Accessories: Fairy wings

Magical powers: Shakespearian enchantments

Realms: Vonderland

Relationship: Conjured by BORGE and LUCREZIA from a book of plays

Adventures: BORGE and LUCREZIA are disappointed not to be cast in the Vonderland production of Shakespeare's *A Midsummer Night's Dream*. To get their own back, they conjure up the real PUCK – a character from the play. But the twins discover that the mischievous sprite is more than they can handle …

ROLAND DARTMOOR

Being: Warlock

Accessories: Very confident personality!

Magical powers: Very advanced skills

Realms: Germany

Relationship: HEADMISTRESS CRYSTALGAZER's nephew – he's filling in while COACH KUBA is on holiday

Adventures: ROLAND DARTMOOR is a real hearthrob. After all, he's three-times SCOOTSOOMER champion of the WWWWF (World Witches, Wizards and Warlocks Federation). As soon as he arrives at Vonderland, students are swooning over his good looks and asking for SCOOTSOOMER tips. But DARTMOOR has a sinister reason for his visit. His great friend ZARLAK has asked him to expel CASSY, GUS and VERNE from Vonderland.

SELKIES

Being: Magical sea lions

Accessories: Trident

Magical powers: Hide their identity magically, fire blasts of magic

Realms: Undersea Realm

Relationship: Led by LORD SELKAR and ZARLAK

Adventures: ZARLAK has given the SELKIES special powers so that they can capture UBOS from CASSY, GUS and VERNE.

SERPENTIUM

Being: Serpent-like creature

Accessories: Razor-sharp teeth and talons

Magical powers: Can fly

Realms: LOGIKUS NULL

Relationship: ZARLAK's servant

Adventures: SERPENTIUM is the keeper of LOGIKUS NULL. It's his job to guard the Dark Matrix – a glowing pool of logic.

SIEGE PERILOUS

Being: The legendary throne of Sir Galahad

Accessories: Ornate swirls and decorations

Magical powers: Whoever sits in the seat is sent back to their magical roots.

Realms: Vonderland

Relationship: SIEGE PERILOUS is the latest addition to the Vonderland museum.

Adventures: When GUS and CASSY sit in Siege Perilous, CASSY begins to turn to wood (as witches were once said to be) and GUS starts to become a werewolf (like his great-grandfather). There's only one person who can sort out the problem – MERLIN, the greatest wizard of all time.

SPIKE

Being: Huge spike-covered metallic creature

Accessories: Lots of sharp spikes!

Magical powers: Robotic powers

Realms: Cleaver Cusp Realm

Relationship: One of ZARLAK's servants

Adventures: SPIKE tries to catch CASSY, GUS and VERNE when they come looking for the sharp things that have vanished from Surface World.

   On their next trip, when they are searching for Excalibur, they end up actually inside SPIKE!

TARL

Being: Ganesha – elephant-like creature

Accessories: Weapon in holster

Magical powers: None

Realms: World of the Imps

Relationship: ZARLAK's tax collector

Adventures: It's TARL's job to gather money for ZARLAK. CASSY, GUS and VERNE come across the great creature in the Scavenger Imp Realm, when he's searching for a portal for his master – ZARLAK.

TUSKUS

Being: SELKIE

Accessories: None

Magical powers: Hides his identity magically, fires blasts of magic

Realms: Undersea Realm

Relationship: Second in command to LORD SELKAR

Adventures: TUSKUS steals Cassy's backpack when she is lured aboard a ghost ship. Will the SELKIES steal UBOS?

WINGO and JINGO

Being: Gremlins

Accessories: None

Magical powers:
Shape-shifting and other mischievous magic

Realms: Vonderland

Relationship: Brother and sister

Adventures: WINGO and JINGO love to play tricks on each other – and on everyone else. CASSY, GUS and VERNE arrive back from Centre Earth one night, to discover that the gremlins are creating havoc at Vonderland – while everyone else is in an enchanted sleep. They must reverse the sleeping spell, or no one will wake for the next hundred years ...

WYRMOST

Being: Dragon

Accessories: Sleeps perched on a pile of Changeling crystals

Magical powers: Breathes fire and can fly

Realms: Centre Earth

Relationship: ZARLAK's enemy

Adventures: Almost as much trouble as ZARLAK, WYRMOST was banished by the Wizards' High Council to Centre Earth long ago. When CASSY, GUS, VERNE and GEZ try to escape from Centre Earth without UBOS's help, CASSY tries to persuade WYRMOST to let them through his gateway into the next realm – to defeat ZARLAK.

ZOG

Being: Troll queen

Accessories: Handbag

Magical powers:
Transforms herself into a raven

Realms:
Umbra, Fornax

Relationship: ZOG is madly in love with ZARLAK.

Adventures: ZOG will do anything to make ZARLAK fall in love with her. She will steal the magic of laughter from the world, steal bubbles to cleanse ZARLAK of the enchantment that traps him in Centre Earth, steal CUPID's bow ... And all because she wants to be his beloved queen.

BAD REALMS

CAVE OF NEVERIA

Features: Wormwood Dungeon

Dwellers: Dozens of bats hanging from the ceiling

Magical objects: Tear of Moolana

Adventures: The Cave of Neveria holds a tear-shaped diamond that contains the magic of Supreme Sorceress Moolana. MASTER WIZARD VALENTINE tells the students that whoever owns this gem will become immensely powerful. CASSY and GUS can't resist the lure of the Tear of Moolana, but VERNE thinks it's all a trick ...

CLEAVER CUSP REALM

Features: A realm filled with huge spikes and jagged blades

Dwellers: SPIKE, ZOG

Magical objects:
Excalibur (King Arthur's sword)

Adventures: The Cleaver Cusp Realm is where ZARLAK takes all of the sharp things from Surface World. He wants to make the Mortie-Muds dull — so he'll be able to move in and take over without a fight. This is also the place where ZOG traps the world's bubbles. Her aim is to cleanse ZARLAK of the enchantment that keeps him in Centre Earth — and win his heart.

LOGIKUS NULL

Features: The Dark Matrix — a glowing pool of logic

Dwellers: Serpentium

Magical objects: Square Root Amulet of Logikos Null — makes every spell work in reverse

Adventures: ZARLAK uses the magical amulet to draw logic down to Centre Earth, and is helped in his task by SERPENTIUM. Without computers or magic, Surface World will be useless! To restore the world's logic, CASSY, GUS and VERNE brave the never-ending stairs of LOGIKUS NULL — a place where you have to go up, if you want to go down …

BAD REALMS

REALM OF WYRMOST

Features: Chamber of Bacchanalia

Dwellers: WYRMOST, Elementals – flame creatures

Magical objects: Elvenstone, Changeling crystal

Adventures: The great dragon, WYRMOST, guards the Elvenstone – the gem that gives all elves their power. Changeling crystals can also be found in this realm. GUS desperately wants a crystal so that he can turn lead into gold and really impress his parents.

ROOTOPIA

Features: A bizarre underground world filled with roots

Dwellers: GARDEN GNOMES

Magical objects: Rapunzel plant, gnome thistle, ostrich root plant

Adventures: The GARDEN GNOMES are under ZARLAK's control, yanking the TALKING FLOWERS and other plants down into Rootopia by their roots. The Supreme Wizard knows that without the magic of living things, Surface Earth cannot survive. CASSY, GUS and VERNE must take part in a daring Rootopia rescue.

SHADOWLAND

Features: One of the gloomiest levels in Centre Earth

Dwellers: GALK, GIANT ONE-EYED OGRE

Magical objects: Giant crystal cauldron – the portal to Whimsy Way

Adventures: When CASSY, GUS and VERNE's shadows are stolen, they are held captive in a crystal cylinder in Shadowland. Whimsy Way – the place where imaginary creatures go when children get tired of them – can be reached through Shadowland.

TOADSTOOL REALM

Features: Crystalline Forest

Dwellers: ZARLAK, ROWCE and SNERRAT

Magical objects: Giant toadstools

Adventures: This is the first realm that CASSY, GUS and VERNE visit on their many trips to Centre Earth. It's the place where UBOS explains their mission and also where VERNE first amazes everyone (including himself) with his magical skills.

TROLL REALM

Features:
Fortress Swamp

Dwellers:
Rock trolls, gold trolls, buckskin trolls, shoe-stealing trolls…

Magical objects:
None

Adventures:
Trolls help ZARLAK by kidnapping ELSA and taking her down into the Troll Realm. There, ZARLAK waits for CASSY, GUS and VERNE to rescue her. He is ready to trap them and steal UBOS!

UMBRA

Features:
Fairy Penal Colony

Dwellers:
ZOG, GOODY TOOTHPICKS

Magical objects:
Swirling vortex that reaches into the sky

Adventures:
Also known as the Level of the Eternal Eclipse, UMBRA is a dark, shadowy place. This is the home of GOODY TOOTHPICKS, who turned ERBERT into a toy. To punish CASSY and GUS, she changes them into toads for her toad stew!

BAD REALMS

UNDERSEA REALM

Features: The KRAKEN prison

Dwellers: SHIMMARYN, SELKIE GUARDS, Ulupies – sea serpents with human faces, Grogans – froglike creatures with kind eyes and moustaches

Magical objects:
A towering rock dome that is more than meets the eye. Really, it is KRAKEN – its body is the dome, its tentacles the pillars.

Adventures: When CASSY, GUS and VERNE travel to this realm, they are all given gills (by UBOS and LORD SELKAR), so that they can breathe underwater. Then they must free the sea creatures held captive by the SELKIES.

UNDERWORLD SWAMP REALM

Features: Misty swamps

Dwellers: Slime Rooters – small, pink, wriggly, sausage-shaped creatures; ONE-EYED GIANT SWAMP SLUG BEAST

Magical objects:
Slime Rooters!

Adventures: A dash of magic gunk from the belly of a Slime Rooter and – hey presto – you're cured of ZARLAK's crash bug! CASSY, GUS and VERNE visit the Underworld Swamp Realm to find them, but they don't reckon on having to get past the ONE-EYED GIANT SWAMP SLUG BEAST...

WORLD OF THE IMPS

Features: Filled with weird shapes and fairground mirrors

Dwellers: Imps

Magical objects: Imp bottles – each is home to an imp

Adventures: SCRIMPY travels to Vonderland to ask for CASSY's help when ZARLAK threatens the imps. She, GUS and VERNE whizz down to the World of the Imps to set the imps free. But, in the World of the Imps, nothing is as it seems …

ZARLAK'S REALM

Features: Zarlak's castle (with its moat of molten lava)

Dwellers: ZARLAK , ROWCE and SNERRAT

Magical objects: Crystal ball, flying throne, magical cauldron

Adventures: At the very core of Centre Earth, there lies a realm more dangerous than any other – Zarlak's Realm. Here, in his dark and gloomy castle, Zarlak conjures up ways to steal enough magic to escape from Centre Earth. Will CASSY, GUS and VERNE be able to stop the Supreme Wizard from taking over the whole world?

INDEX

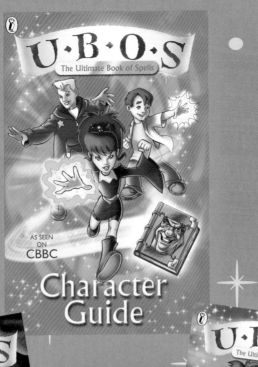

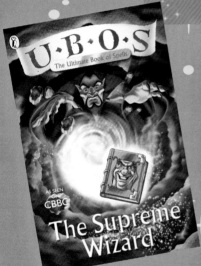

The magic is here . . .

AS SEEN
ON
CBBC

U·B·O·S

The Ultimate Magic Video

Yours To Own on Video

Available From All Good Retailers

AS SEEN ON
CBBC

U·B·O·S

The Ultimate
Book of Spells

VOLUME
I

THREE IS A CHARM

UNIVERSAL

VHS

UBOS™ & © 2001 BKN International AG. All rights reserved